About This Book

Title: *Eel Hides*

Step: 5

Word Count: 399

Skills in Focus: ee, -ey

Tricky Words: another, both, could, first, forever, grouper, moray eel, sometimes, success, timidly, told

Ideas for Using this Book

Before Reading:
- **Comprehension:** Take a picture walk through the book. Have readers make predictions or make connections to what they see. Have them give specific examples from their observations.
- **Phonics:** Tell the students they will read words with the long e sound, /ē/. The pattern *ee* makes this sound as well as *ey* at the end of a word. Write both patterns on the board. Offer story words *eel* and *Finley* as an example for each pattern, underlining the target letter(s) in each word. Practice blending the sounds in the words. Have students take a quick walk through the first few pages of text to identify additional words with long *e* pattern (i.e. *see, weeks, between*).
- **Vocabulary:** Briefly explain that *keen* means extreme or very strong (like a sense of smell or eyesight), *sleek* means smooth, and to *screech* means to shout in a loud, high voice.

During Reading:
- Have the readers use their fingers to track the words as they read if needed.
- **Decoding:** If stuck on a word, help readers say each sound and blend it together smoothly.
- **Comprehension:** Look closely at the facts found on the first page of text. Prompt readers to look for story events that support the facts about moray eels.

After Reading:
Discuss the book. Some ideas for questions:
- Why was Finley good at hiding?
- Why was Finley scared of Reese?
- Explain how Finley changed throughout the story. What caused him to change?
- Why did Reese think Finley would make a good hunting buddy?
- What lesson might Finley have learned?

Eel Hides

Text by
Leanna Koch

Educational Content by
Kristen Cowen

Illustrated by
Steve Harpster

PICTURE WINDOW BOOKS
a capstone imprint

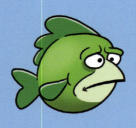

FINLEY THE MORAY EEL

Five Moray Eel Facts:

1. Moray eels are fish that look like snakes.

2. Moray eels can go for weeks without eating.

3. Moray eels may team up with other fish to hunt.

4. Moray eels like to hide in cracks and rocky spaces.

5. Moray eels cannot see well but have a keen sense of smell.

Finley the eel liked to
play hide-and-seek.

He was the best hider
on the reef.

Finley could slide his skinny
body into thin cracks.

The reef fish could not see him.

The rest of the reef fish
got hungry and gave up.

Finley didn't need to eat each day. He could go three weeks with no food.

Soon the rest of the reef fish were keeping busy with one new hobby or another. They did not want to play hide-and-seek.

Then a new fish came to the reef,
a big grouper named Reese.

Reese had pretty spots and plenty of teeth. She was chatty and made fast friends.

Finley hid in his cave. He did not like the looks of Reese's teeth.

A big fish like Reese
might eat eels.

Finley hid in his cave
for three weeks.

Then Reese came to Finley's cave. "Hi, buddy!" Reese said.

Finley hid. He was glad that
Reese did not fit in his cave.

Finley wished he could
keep hidden forever,
but he got hungry.

He peeked out of his cave.

Reese was right there.
"Hi, buddy!" she said.

"Please don't eat me!"
Finley screeched.

"That's funny!" Reese said.
"You are way too big to
eat! Let me see you."

Finley slid from his cave. "Look at those pretty spots and that sleek body!" Reese said.

"Gee, thanks! I like your spots, too," said Finley.

"You have nice teeth and a keen sense of smell. You seem to be just right," Reese said.

"Just right?" Finley asked.

"I need a hunting buddy," Reese replied.

"I've never had a hunting buddy!"
Finley said.

"We will be the best team on the reef," Reese told Finley. Finley was happy to have a new friend.

Finley and Reese were a good
team. They got a lot of food.
Finley liked hunting with Reese.

Both fish liked having a full belly. "I can sleep for weeks after this feast," Finley said to Reese.

"Want to play hide-and-seek first?" Reese asked.

"Yes!" Finley cheered.

More Ideas:

Making words with ee:

Tell the readers you will say a story word with the long *e* sound made by the vowel team *ee*. Begin by having the students write the word *see*, s-ee. Then, tell the readers they will change either the initial or ending sound to make a new word. Ask the students to change the word *see* to *seem* (add an *m* to the end). Readers can point to the written letters as they slowly segment the new word to help identify the changing sound. Continue adding or substituting sounds to make a new *ee* word.

Suggested words:
  see, seem, seek, peek, week, sleek,
  sleep, keep, keen, between

Extended Learning Activity

Compare and Contrast Characters

At first, Finley feared Reese, but he eventually realized they weren't so different. Think about what makes these characters alike and different. Write one or more ways they are similar and one or more ways they differ. Option to use a graphic organizer to record ideas.

Finley-Different	Same	Reese-Different

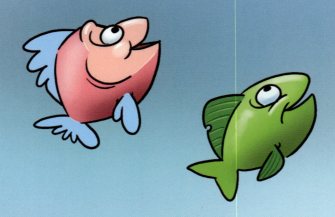

Published by Picture Window Books,
an imprint of Capstone
1710 Roe Crest Drive,
North Mankato, Minnesota 56003
capstonepub.com

Eel Hides was originally published as
The Hiding Eel copyright 2012 by Stone Arch Books.

Library of Congress Cataloging-in-Publication Data is available
on the Library of Congress website.

ISBN: 9780756595524 (hardback)
ISBN: 9780756585822 (paperback)
ISBN: 9780756590765 (eBook PDF)

Printed and bound in the USA. 5757